RED STAR LINE.
FIRST CABIN.
WANTED ON VOYAGE

Name...Sailing...........................

Stateroom...

THE LUCK OF THE LOCH NESS MONSTER

A TALE OF PICKY EATING

A.W. FLAHERTY

ILLUSTRATED BY SCOTT MAGOON

Houghton Mifflin Company • Boston 2007

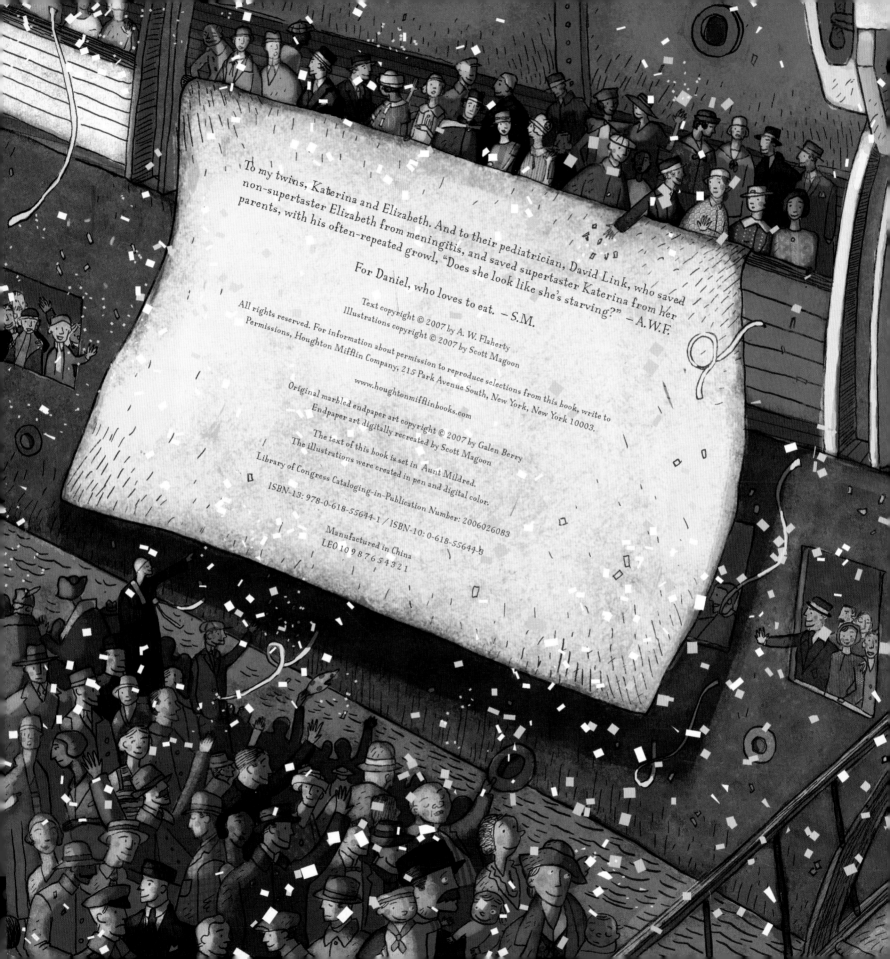

To my twins, Katerina and Elizabeth. And to their pediatrician, David Link, who saved non-supertaster Elizabeth from meningitis, and saved supertaster Katerina from her parents, with his often-repeated growl, "Does she look like she's starving?" —A.W.F.

For Daniel, who loves to eat. —S.M.

Text copyright © 2007 by A. W. Flaherty
Illustrations copyright © 2007 by Scott Magoon

www.houghtonmifflinbooks.com

Original marbled endpaper art copyright © 2007 by Galen Berry.
Endpaper art digitally recreated by Scott Magoon.

The text of this book is set in Aunt Mildred.
The illustrations were created in pen and digital color.

Library of Congress Cataloging-in-Publication Number: 2006026083

ISBN-13: 978-0-618-55644-1 / ISBN-10: 0-618-55644-3

Manufactured in China
LEO 10 9 8 7 6 5 4 3 2 1

Once upon a time, a little girl named Katerina-Elizabeth took an ocean liner to visit her grandmother in Scotland. It was the first time she had traveled by herself.

Her parents had thoughtfully planned every step of her trip for her, even her meals. So for breakfast the first day, Katerina-Elizabeth found a bowl of gray gooey oatmeal, her least favorite food in the world.

Her parents always told her that without oatmeal she would grow up stunted.

She threw it out the porthole.

The oatmeal sank in a lump to the bottom of the sea.
By luck, it landed next to a tiny sea worm, no bigger
around than a thread and no longer than your
thumbnail. The sea worm had never seen anything as
lovely as the oatmeal.

ACTUAL
SIZE!

It

gobbled

it

up.

By the time it finished eating, it was as thick
as yarn and as long as your hand.

ACTUAL
SIZE!

It decided to follow the ship.

The next morning, Katerina-Elizabeth watched
the other diners enjoying cinnamon rolls with icing.
But for Katerina-Elizabeth, it was oatmeal again.

She threw it out the porthole.

And grabbed a cinnamon roll.

Again, the oatmeal sank like lead. The worm gobbled it up. It grew even larger, as long as your whole body. Then it swallowed the bowl, too.

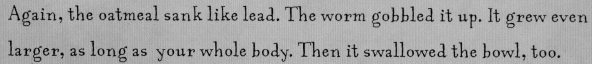

NOT ACTUAL SIZE!

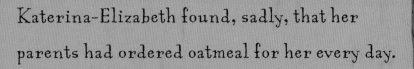

Katerina-Elizabeth found, sadly, that her parents had ordered oatmeal for her every day.

Soon the delighted worm learned to swim right under the porthole at breakfast and to catch her oatmeal in midair.

The worm surprised Katerina-Elizabeth the first time she saw it. She did not especially like snaky things.

She began to change her mind, however, when she realized how quickly the worm learned tricks.

When the ship reached Scotland, it
continued up the River Ness to Loch Ness.
The worm followed.

Katerina-Elizabeth was glad to escape the boat to stay with her grandmother (who had been born in the Ukraine and did not know how to make oatmeal).

But the worm cried.

Anxious to find more oatmeal, the worm circled Loch Ness. Luckily, oatmeal is the national breakfast food of Scotland, and as many Scottish children hate it as American ones do. All along the lake the next morning, the worm heard the plop of oatmeal being hurled by children out the windows of their thatched cottages and into the lake.

All that summer the sea worm—now a lake worm—made morning rounds of the lake to salvage the children's oatmeal.

PLOP!

After a few months, a child leaving her house early one
morning saw the worm plowing through the water.
"Hey, a monster!" she shouted.
The worm was about to politely correct the child,
but first looked at its reflection in the water.
The worm saw that it had changed a great deal
since its first bite of oatmeal.

It was now as thick as an elephant's belly and as long as the main hall of an elementary school. It had sleek scales, an imposing row of fins down its back, and white teeth that were quite sharp, perhaps because nothing tougher than oatmeal had ever worn them down.

The worm, now the monster, was thrilled with its home in Loch Ness. It found that there were other Scottish foods that children often tossed in the lake—such as haggis, and suet pudding. It grew fond of them, too.

The monster was lucky that it loved Loch Ness, because by then it was too big to swim down the river and back to the sea. Sometimes, though, the monster worried about the future. What if all the children moved away?

Being an American worm, however, it knew the usefulness of
advertising, and occasionally it allowed itself to be seen at dawn.
Soon tourists flocked to Loch Ness.

BEAST OF THE DEEP

Loch Ness Scotland

SEE LOCH NESS

ADMIT ONE 1

Scotland Times

WHAT IS IT?
MONSTER SPOTTED
IN LOCH NESS,
NICKNAMED "NESSIE"

MYSTERIOUS CREATURE

Many rode the morning tour boats, hoping to see "Nessie,"

and while waiting, they ordered the national dish.

After a few bites, they, too, would discreetly throw it overboard.

At the end of Nessie's first summer, the most famous
Loch Ness Monster sighting occurred as a big ship
was leaving for America. To the amazement of all,
the monster rose from the deep, arched its neck,
and kissed a small American child named
Katerina-Elizabeth on the nose.

Despite her parents' warning about the importance of oatmeal, Katerina-Elizabeth lived happily ever after.

DON'T FEED THE BIRDS

RED STAR LINE

Breakfast

Oranges   Apples
Milkrice Oatmeal
Broiled Sardines on toast
Salt Mackerel
Kippered herring
Pork Chops a la Soubise
Red pepper veal steak
Mutton chops
Cornedbeef hash with egg
Beefsteak, broiled and fried
Yorkshire ham & bacon
French fried potatoes
Saratoga chips
Scrambled eggs
Eggs au gratin
Omelet aux morilles
Hominy & buckwheat cakes
Cold: Beeftongue sausage
Marmalade

Biscuits Rolls Crescents
Tea Coffee· Cocoa Chocolate
Cream   Fresh Milk

It was true, though, that she grew up to be three inches shorter than everyone else in her family.

ABSTRACT OF LOG.

Triple-Screw R.M.S. "OLYMPIA" 46,439 Tons.

Commander: I. DAHLIN, C.B., D.S.O., R.D. (Commodore R.N.R.)

VOYAGE NO. 117 EAST

NEW YORK TO LOCH NESS VIA BELFAST.

Took departure from Ambrose Channel L.V. at 8 AM (E.S.T.), June 29, 1925

Remarks.

The Science of It All

When I was little, my father told a version of this monster story to get me to eat my oatmeal. Although I loved the story, it didn't make me eat. Now I have twin girls, one of whom is a picky eater like me, the other a normal eater like my husband. That got me interested in the biology of pickiness. My husband has so far kept me from doing experiments on my children.

People often blame picky eating on children's willfulness. Much pickiness is genetic, though, and sometimes even helps children stay healthy. Most picky eaters have a gene called Supertaster. If you have both copies of the gene, you taste flavors strongly, especially bitter compounds in foods like broccoli. Yuck. If you have neither copy, you can't taste those bitter flavors at all.

"Hey!" you say. "Isn't broccoli supposed to help prevent cancer?" Sure, because those same bitter compounds kill fast-growing cancer cells. But the compounds may even hurt the fast-growing cells of children. Children don't get cancer as often as old people do, so I say that children should get to give their broccoli to their grandparents.

Finicky eaters tend to be smaller than their brothers and sisters. It turns out, though, that they were just as much smaller at birth as they are later—their smallness began before their pickiness. And picky eaters are less likely to get fat or have heart attacks later. Is that so bad?

SUPERTASTER TEST: Are you a supertaster? It's easy to tell, because supertasters have more taste buds. You'll need blue food coloring, a cotton swab, and a reinforcing ring for three-holed paper. With the cotton swab, dab a little food coloring on the front of your tongue. Put the ring over it and count the number of taste buds inside the ring. Supertasters have more than thirty, nontasters less than fifteen, and average tasters are in between.

LOCH NESS MONSTER TEST: As for scientific evidence that the Loch Ness Monster exists, I'm afraid space doesn't permit going into that here.